THE
Sea Monster's
SECRET

MALKA DRUCKER

illustrated by CHRISTOPHER AJA

GULLIVER BOOKS/HARCOURT BRACE & COMPANY · *San Diego   New York   London*

For Ivan, with love
—M. D.

For my parents, Gilbert and Leslie
—C. A.

Library of Congress Cataloging-in-Publication Data
Drucker, Malka.
The sea monster's secret/Malka Drucker; illustrated by Christopher Aja.
p. cm.
"Gulliver Books."
Summary: A young man proves himself to be resourceful and brave, despite the mockery of his nagging
mother-in-law, when he wears the skin of a ferocious sea monster he has slain.
ISBN 0-15-200619-2
1. Tlingit Indians—Folklore. 2. Haida Indians—Folklore. 3. Tales—Alaska. 4. Tales—British Columbia.
[1. Tlingit Indians—Folklore. 2. Haida Indians—Folklore. 3. Indians of North America—Northwest, Pacific—Folklore.]
I. Aja, Christopher, ill. II. Title. III. Series.
E99.T6D78 1999
398.24'54'0899720795
[E]—dc20 96-5123

First edition
A C E F D B
Printed in Hong Kong

The illustrations in this book were painted
with acrylics and gouache on illustration board.
The display type was set in OptiMarcus.
The text type was set in Deepdene.
Color separations by Bright Arts Ltd., Hong Kong
Printed by South China Printing Company, Ltd., Hong Kong
This book was printed on totally chlorine-free Nymolla Matte Art paper.
Production supervision by Stanley Redfern and Pascha Gerlinger
Designed by Lisa Peters

ONCE, LONG AGO, when unseen spirits filled the world and giant fish filled the sea, a handsome young man traveled from his home to a neighboring village. There he married a beautiful and wellborn young woman and moved into her family's home by the seashore. The young man and young woman were very happy, but the young man's mother-in-law was not pleased. "He's the laziest thing I've ever seen!" she told her daughter time and time again.

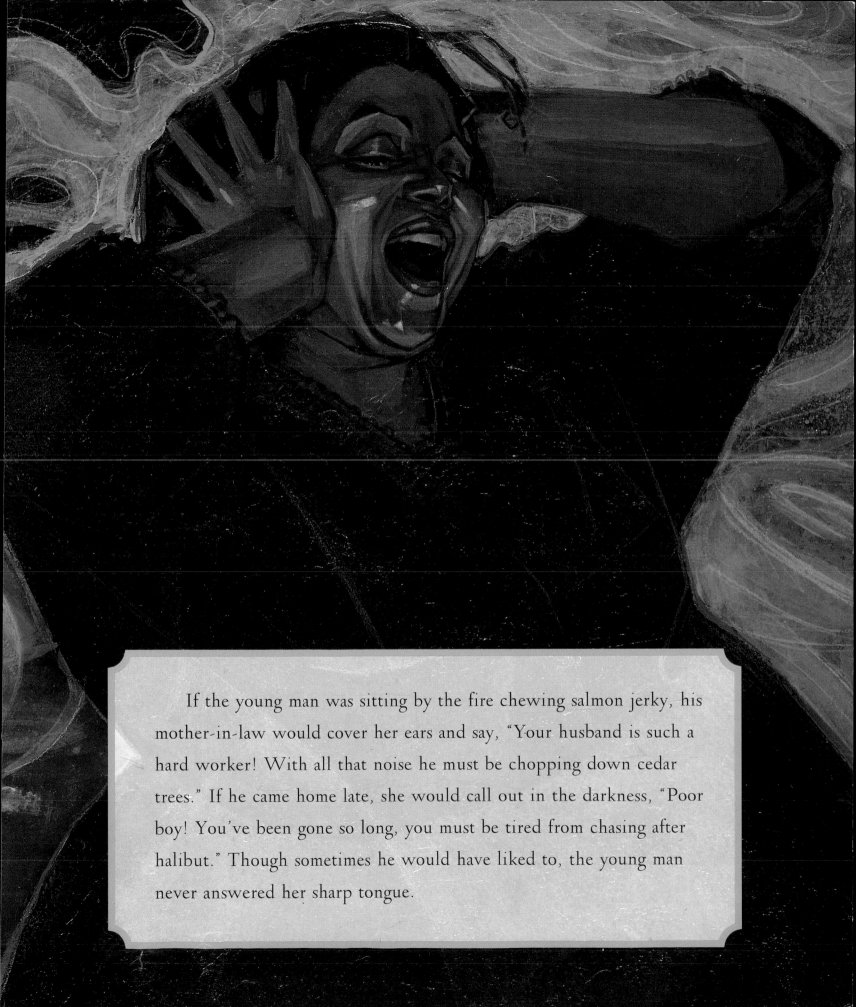

If the young man was sitting by the fire chewing salmon jerky, his mother-in-law would cover her ears and say, "Your husband is such a hard worker! With all that noise he must be chopping down cedar trees." If he came home late, she would call out in the darkness, "Poor boy! You've been gone so long, you must be tired from chasing after halibut." Though sometimes he would have liked to, the young man never answered her sharp tongue.

One evening when he couldn't stand his mother-in-law's nagging voice, the young man left the house. Ever since he had come to his wife's village, he had heard about a sapphire-clear bay surrounded by fat cedar trees. Although the bay was not far, no one visited it—some whispered stories about people who'd gone there and never returned. Others said a monster lived at its bottom. Eager to be alone, the young man set off for the bay, taking with him only an ax he had honed to the sharpest edge.

As he approached the bay, he heard nothing but silence. No creature stirred, no wind blew. But it was as beautiful as everyone had said.

The young man decided to find out for himself if he had come to a monster's home. Using a thick cedar tree and a small but strong alder sapling, he made a trap. Then he took a piece of salmon jerky from his pocket, attached it to the alder wood, and gently slipped the baited trap into the bay.

The young man waited. Soon the quiet water began to bubble around the trap. A gleaming black mass broke the surface of the moonlit water. The sea monster! Although the young man had hunted and fished all his life, this was the strangest creature he had ever seen. As the sea monster bit down on the salmon, the alder wood snapped, springing the trap and killing the monster instantly.

The young man dragged the sea monster out of the water,
gutted the beast, and dried the skin. He ran his hand over it
and pressed it to his face. Its strange beauty called to him, and
he wrapped it around himself. To his surprise, the enormous
skin fit him snugly. Just then the young man felt a tug.

Suddenly the young man found himself in the bay, swimming underwater, seeing perfectly and breathing like a fish. The skin was taking him back to its home. When he reached the bottom of the bay, the young man saw that he had entered a splendid underwater hall decorated with intricately carved wood and brightly painted boxes. He felt oddly at home in this silent, peaceful place.

Eventually, thinking of his gentle bride, the young man returned to the shore. He took off the sea monster's skin, folded it carefully, and put it in the hollow of a tree. He understood that possessing a magic skin could be useful.

When he returned home, his mother-in-law looked at his empty hands and laughed. "Are you hiding some salmon outside, son-in-law? Or perhaps a nice fat seal?"

Hungry and tired from his underwater journey, the young man smiled wearily and shook his head. "Next time, mother-in-law," he said.

"Instead of a provider, I have an extra mouth to feed!" she complained.

That evening when the sun set, the young man returned to
the hollow of the tree and slipped into the sea monster's skin.
Stepping into the water, he felt the skin pull him down toward
the sea monster's hall, but this time he swam beyond it and
followed a current that led into the sea. The water grew colder
and the fish grew bigger.

When a large silver salmon swam by, the young man caught
the fish in his powerful jaws. Inside the skin, he smiled.

When the young man returned to the shore, he was surprised
to see it was dawn. He took off the skin, folded it, and put it back
in the hollow of the tree. Then he carried the shining fish back to
the village and left it outside his mother-in-law's door before
going in to bed.

When the mother-in-law opened her door in the morning and saw the salmon, she thought it had washed up from the sea. She showed it to her husband, exclaiming over her good luck. That night the woman and her daughter cleaned and cooked the fish, and the family feasted on the magnificent salmon. Wearing a grand robe for the occasion, the mother-in-law remarked, "This good fortune makes up for other disappointments," and looked pointedly at the young man.

That night, after everyone else was asleep and dreaming of their salmon dinner, the young man went to the hollow of the tree and put on the skin again. This time it carried him into even deeper waters in the sea. When a halibut twice the size of a seal swam by, he easily snared it with his powerful fin-claws. After swimming back to the bay, he took off the skin and lugged the halibut to his mother-in-law's door.

"Come! Look at this!" his mother-in-law shrieked in the morning. "The spirits of the sea have answered my prayers!" Her shouts awakened the young man. He chuckled to himself and went back to sleep.

Again that night there was a feast, and again when everyone else was asleep, the young man slipped out to hunt. He swam for a long time before a great shadow passed in front of him. It was a killer whale—the fiercest of beasts. The whale fought hard but was no match for the sea monster.

In the morning the mother-in-law found the whale, fat enough to feed a hundred people, by the door. Her ecstatic screeches could be heard throughout the village. "We will have a feast such as no one has ever seen before!" she promised.

The whole village was invited to the feast, but when the villagers gathered for the celebration two evenings later, no one recognized the mother-in-law. Her face was covered with a Food-Finding-Spirit mask and she had dressed herself as a shaman, one who is close to the mystery and magic of the world.

She was especially happy that night because her son-in-law was nowhere to be found. *Maybe I've finally driven him away,* she thought. She began to dream of a new match for her daughter, making a list in her mind of eligible young men from good families well-known for their skill in hunting.

The feast went on all night, with the villagers sighing and moaning with delight. The "shaman" had just begun a speech applauding herself for having powers to bring food from the sea, when there was a thud at the door.

The young man's father-in-law stood up, but before he could move,

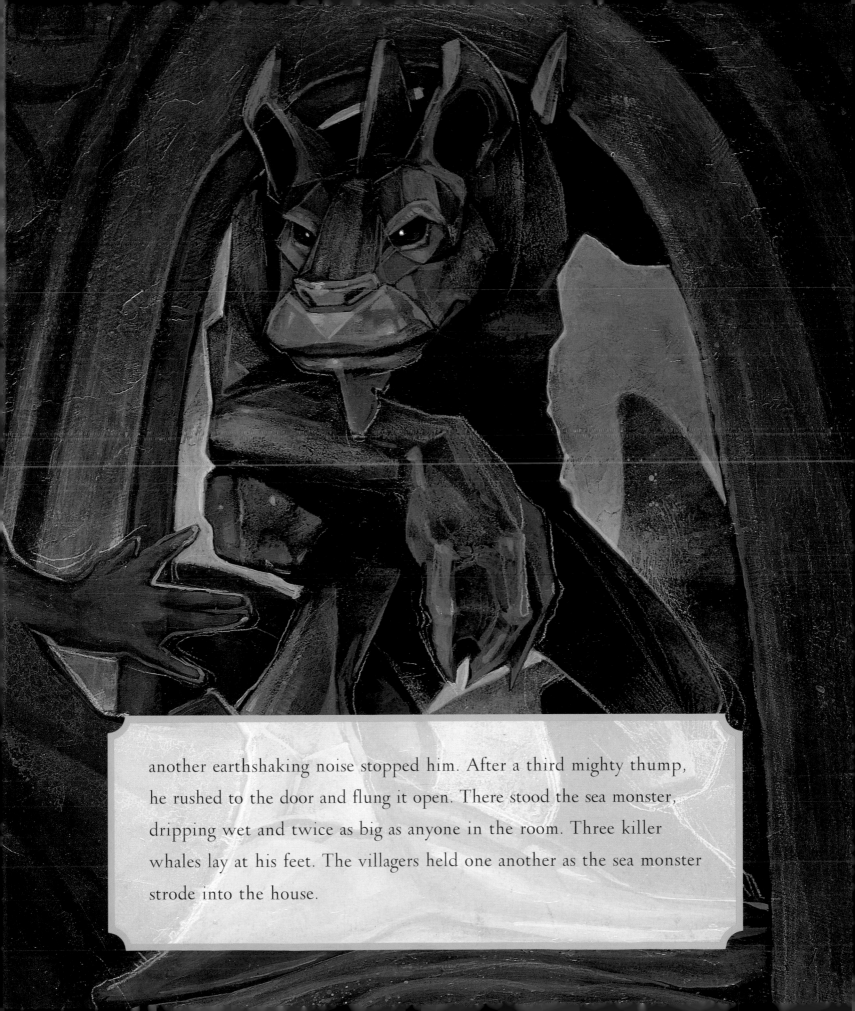

another earthshaking noise stopped him. After a third mighty thump, he rushed to the door and flung it open. There stood the sea monster, dripping wet and twice as big as anyone in the room. Three killer whales lay at his feet. The villagers held one another as the sea monster strode into the house.

He pushed past the old man and the old woman and walked over to their daughter. When the young woman looked up at the huge black eyes of the beast, she almost laughed. In those eyes she recognized her husband!

"Look, Mother! Here is your magic power! It's my husband!"

But the old woman didn't hear her daughter's words. She had run from the house, and no one has seen her since.

No one has ever called the young man lazy again. And winter or summer, the village has always had plenty to eat.

STORYTELLER'S NOTE

USUALLY WE COME to know a story by hearing or reading it, but I learned about the sea monster from a silent storyteller that stood sixty feet high. I was near Ketchikan, Alaska, in Mud Bight, a re-creation of a traditional native village built where the Tlingit people once lived. Fourteen sixty-foot, brightly colored, and intricately carved totem poles face the water. Three hundred years ago the Tlingits built totem poles like these to pass their history and legends on from generation to generation.

Traditionally a totem pole was carved from a straight, tall, soft-wooded tree, usually a cedar. Once the carver knew which story the owner wanted to tell, he sketched a design on the tree. The artist had only a narrow curved surface on which to carve, so most figures were long and skinny. Despite having very little space, he had to carve enough of the figures so everyone would understand the story. When the carving was finished, he painted the pole with vivid paints made from clamshells, lichen, copper pebbles, berries, and salmon eggs. Often a carver took a year to complete a totem pole.

Of all the totem poles in Mud Bight, I found the sea monster pole most fascinating. So many faces and so many pairs of eyes stared at me from top to bottom. Who were they? As I learned, the faces belonged to characters from the story of the sea monster.

Like a poem, a totem pole hints at much more than it actually says, so after I left Mud Bight I looked for—and found—several written versions of the sea monster story. The Tlingits and their neighbors, the Haida, told this story, though not always with the same ending. In some versions the young man dies when he tries to bring back more than one whale; in others the young man is successful in his attempt. I prefer the second ending and have used it.

Perhaps one day you will have the chance to see totem poles in their original settings. There, in the forest by the sea, look at these tall columns of memory. Remember this story, and imagine the world of a people who carved the men and women, animals and spirits of the totem poles.